A CASE MOST PERSONAL

CONNOR WHITELEY

No part of this book may be reproduced in any form or by any electronic or mechanical means. Including information storage, and retrieval systems, without written permission from the author except for the use of brief quotations in a book review.

This book is NOT legal, professional, medical, financial or any type of official advice.

Any questions about the book, rights licensing, or to contact the author, please email connorwhiteley@connorwhiteley.net

Copyright © 2023 CONNOR WHITELEY

All rights reserved.

DEDICATION

Thank you to all my readers without you I couldn't do what I love.

CHAPTER 1
16th June 2022

Canterbury, England

Private Eye Bettie English might not have been a university student that seemed to flood the city's high street every night, but she always loved, appreciated and respected them.

She was once a student a few decades ago and she spend her time partying, drinking and enjoying the opposite sex. But those days were long behind her.

As Bettie laid on her new sofa bed in her office just above Canterbury high street, Bettie loved listening to the late night talking and laughing of students and the soft music playing from local bars and clubs. There was something so innocent about it that Bettie just loved, and whilst she had no idea why she was still in her office ten o'clock at night. She was enjoying her time.

The wonderful smell of Italian food, rich bitter

coffee and the most amazing vanilla cakes from the local restaurants filled the air and filtered through the office's slightly opened windows to reach Bettie. That was one of the reasons why she loved the high street, it always had the most amazing smells that always left a symphony of flavour on her tongue.

A quiet coughing sound made Bettie raise her head and blew her amazing boyfriend Detective graham Adams a kiss as he gently rubbed her feet after a very busy day of running background checks for various companies.

That was definitely one of the amazing advantages of being pregnant. If Bettie asked for something, she would normally get it like a foot rub or a wonderful vegan dinner.

After being pregnant for so long, Bettie was really started to enjoy vegan food, considering her body couldn't handle the smell, look or even taste of animal products. Including meat, but Bettie loved being pregnant with her twins, one boy, one girl.

And that's what tonight was meant to be about. Bettie had asked Graham to come over after work, they would have dinner in her office and discuss baby names.

Bettie wasn't sure she was going to enjoy it earlier in the day, but during dinner Bettie and Graham had been throwing around silly or even stupid names with each other.

That had been great fun.

Bettie wasn't a fan of Eli, Lincoln or Isaac,

because it would make the baby sound old. And Bettie was never ever going to call their son Ernie, that was a stupidly old name. Graham had completely agreed.

When Bettie noticed that Graham had stopped rubbing her feet, she sat upright, closed the window and snuggled into the beautiful man she loved. Graham was the most beautiful man Bettie had ever seen with his brown hair, fit body and strong cheekbones.

He was pure perfection.

Graham wrapped his arms round Bettie and that's when she noticed that the high street was oddly quiet. But all that meant was it had been ages since Bettie had stayed this late in the office, and now all the students had gone into the restaurants or moved onto the clubs for the night.

"I think we should forget about girl names," Bettie said.

Graham kissed her head. "Thank god. Let's pick a boy's names. We only have a few months until you go pop,"

Bettie playfully hit him. He knew she didn't like that going pop language.

"What about Ronnie?" Bettie asked, smiling.

"Seriously Bet," Graham said, laughing.

"Ronnie can be a rather wonderful name,"

Graham just looked at her.

"Fine," Bettie said, "what Oliver?"

Graham nodded.

"It's a great name. It's posh, distinctive and I knew a few boys called Oliver back in school. They were really hot," Bettie said.

"So you want to call our child after some school crushes?" Graham said, failing to keep his laughter inside.

Bettie half-smiled. Well, he might have had a point. It might be a bit strange but she still really liked the name.

But this whole naming baby stuff was awful. Bettie had heard tons of stories about how children learnt to hate their names, and she absolutely couldn't give their child a name that would get them bullied or joked about for the rest of their lives.

Bettie had no idea how other people decided these. Apparently her sister Phryne had put names into a hat and she picked one out. That's how she named Bettie's wonderful nephew Sean, who Bettie really loved as her own child.

Bettie stood up and looked at the window. With the university year finishing today, she had been expected to see Sean and his Italian boyfriend Harry going out to celebrate. Of course, she knew it was a bit silly to try and see two students out of a sea of them who just swarmed the high street.

But given that Sean was one of the only people Bettie had ever met who managed to pull off very elegant pink highlights in his longish blond hair, Bettie hoped to be able to see him easily.

The entire high street was strangely empty.

From what Bettie could see, there wasn't a single person out now, not even the normal homeless people that Bettie gave leftovers to.

It was almost deadly silent.

Graham yawled and stood up. "Come on mum-to-be, let's get you home. Remember we're going to my mum's tomorrow,"

Bettie rolled her eyes. She couldn't think of anything worse than spending an entire day with Graham's racist, nationalist and homophobic mother. No doubt she would be asking what religion Bettie would be raising the children in (none), she would happening about that "bender" nephew of hers and most importantly she would be asking how many invading foreigners Bettie had dealt with lately.

Bettie hated Graham's mother.

Graham wrapped his arms around her. "I know you don't like her, but-"

"But I want a case so I don't have to go,"

Graham slowly started to kiss her neck. "I'll make it worthwhile,"

Bettie just pointed to the baby bump. "Believe me, I think you've done enough,"

Bettie turned around slowly and kissed Graham. The only reason Bettie wasn't more annoyed at him was because she knew he didn't like his mother either. She wasn't exactly... approving of Bettie, her family and her "bender" nephew.

Bettie wished she was recording his mother when she told him about Sean. Her face was a picture, a very strange and abstract picture of rage, horror and disappointment.

"Auntie!" Sean shouted.

It was coming from outside

Bettie shot up.

She stared out the window.

"Help! Anyone! Please!" Sean shouted.

Bettie saw him. He was carrying someone.

He laid him on the ground.

God! It was Harry.

He had been beaten up.

Then Sean collapsed.

Bettie dashed out the door.

CHAPTER 2
16th June 2022
Canterbury, England

Detective Graham Adams held Bettie tightly in his arms as they stood outside a large hospital room in a very quiet corridor. The corridor itself was nothing special, it was just a long sterile white one with shiny white walls, and Graham hated it.

He had always hated hospitals. It was probably because so many of his family members had died in hospitals alone and unloved. He still hated a lot of his family for various reasons, that was probably why he made sure to love, treasure and love Bettie's family because they had welcomed him so freely when his own family didn't.

The smell of horrible harsh cleaning chemicals filled the hospital with smells of lemons, oranges and cloves. But Graham had seen it all too many times before, and his nose had become accustomed to the true smell of hospitals, all those harsh chemicals did was badly hide the hints of death, urine and blood underneath.

That idea only made Graham hug Bettie tighter.

The entire situation pained Graham more than he wanted to admit, because it was one thing to work an eight-hour shift as a Floater Detective (meaning Graham wasn't tied to any one police department) and see all sorts of evil and crimes.

It was another thing to be off-duty, enjoying time with your sexy girlfriend and then have someone you love being attacked.

But Graham had loved spending time with Bettie. He didn't think he would, after all they were just going to be suggesting baby names to each other. But it was amazing fun. It was wonderful throwing out silly or stupid names and narrowing down what names they wanted.

Graham really wanted to call the boy Zach, Kieran or Ethan. But Bettie wasn't too sure about those names, and Graham wasn't sure about Oliver. It sounded too posh for Canterbury.

So they were at a stalemate. A very fun stalemate.

Graham felt Bettie stand up straight and frown at the hospital room they were outside. That's where the doctors were examining Harry.

At least she had stopped crying out, but Graham didn't really want to see Sean (who was in a hospital room getting stitched up) and Harry (who was... unknown) to remember had beaten they both were.

Graham hated running out onto the high street

seeing all the blood from Sean's stab wound and how bloody and swollen Harry was. Whatever had happened they had been beaten up viciously.

As much as Graham didn't want to admit it, he doubted the only thing the attackers used were fists. They probably used baseball bats, pipes or even rocks.

Graham hissed as he felt his stomach tighten into a painful knot.

Thankfully his friends at the police had agreed to send two officers to interview Sean and Harry and an official investigation would be launched.

Graham was relieved that something would be done after their attack.

After two hours of standing about, Graham was starting to get restless, yet he smiled and felt a massive wave of relief wash over him when he saw two uniformed cops walk past him and nodded at him with respect.

They were being led to Sean by a nurse. That particular nurse (Lucas Bailey) was great, and he had really helped calm down Bettie when they first bought Sean and Harry in.

If anyone could be useful here, it would definitely be that nurse and Graham knew of the two uniformed cops, so hopefully everything would be okay.

"I can't…" Bettie said. "I can't stop seeing Harry's battered body when I close my eyes,"

Graham simply kissed her head and pulled her

close.

"I know. We'll find out what happened," Graham said.

Graham had no idea how Bettie was coping with all this, she was the one who always spent the most time with Sean and Harry. If there was a gay show, pride or theatre thing they wanted to see Bettie would volunteer to go with them. Even though they were over 20 and could drive.

Bettie loved spending time with them, but Graham was more concerned about Sean.

Both Sean and Harry were the cutest, most adorable couple he had ever seen, and Graham never ever spoke like that. They almost eclipsed his own relationship with Bettie, so Graham hated to know what Sean was experiencing.

Then Graham saw the two uniformed cops walk back past with the nurse and they were frowning.

"That's a bit quick," Graham said.

Bettie frowned at the cops.

"They couldn't have taken the statement that quickly. They didn't even see Harry," Graham said.

"Sean!" Bettie shouted, as Sean rolled down the corridor topless but with a massive bandage wrapped tightly round his waist in a wheelchair.

Nurse Lucas raced behind Sean.

Graham really focused on Lucas, and he was a bit surprised to see a really happy looking nurse. Most of the nurses in the NHS looked grumpy, tired and like they didn't want to be there. But Lucas looked so young and happy with his short brown hair, slim body and happy lines covering his entire face.

"Sean," Lucas said, firmly, "you are not meant to leave yet,"

"I have to see him!" Sean said, trying to roll into Harry's hospital room.

Graham grabbed the handles of Sean's wheelchair and he thought Bettie was going to moan at him. She only smiled.

Graham put on the brake and him and Bettie both knelt down so they were eye-level with him.

"Why did the cops leave so quickly?" Bettie asked, a second before Graham could.

Sean just pointed to his longish blond hair with very stylish pink highlights.

"Bastards," Bettie said.

Graham placed his hand on her shoulder and Sean's knee.

"I feared this would happen," Graham said. "They were never going to investigate two young men getting attacked on a party night,"

Graham was almost scared by the look of fury in Bettie's eyes. But it was an extremely outrageous truth that the police were too under-resourced for them to investigate every time young men got into a fight.

Graham gave Sean a half-smile. "Then add in the two young men were gay and one was a foreigner…"

"Yea," Bettie said, "the police were never going to investigate,"

"He isn't a foreigner!" Sean shouted right in

Graham's face. "He dual national!"

Graham wanted to say something to comfort him, but he had no comforting words. At the end of the day, the police were getting better each and every day, but it was nowhere quick enough.

The police were never going to investigate this attack.

And it was clear Sean was furious. Graham wasn't going to blame him or say stupid things like "calm down", because he would have been exactly the same if anything had happened to Bettie.

"Excuse me," Nurse Lucas said behind them.

Graham turned around. "Yes?"

Lucas frowned. "Are any of you family?"

Graham felt like Sean was about to say something but he shot him a warning look.

"Detective-" Graham said.

"Get away from our son's room!" a middle-aged man said in a thick Italian accent.

Graham and Bettie just looked at each other.

Then the man looked at Sean. "You get away from my son, you little bambino gay,"

CHAPTER 3
16th June 2022
Canterbury, England

Bettie had no idea who this idiot was talking to Sean like that. Well, it was clear that this middle-aged Italian man with his salt and pepper hair, slightly large belly and tight business suit was Harry's father. But still!

Bettie just stared at the man as he stared angrily at Sean, like for some reason it was all Sean's fault why his son had been attacked, beaten and was now lying in a hospital bed.

But judging from Sean's face, he had never met Harry's father before, and he almost looked embarrassed now. Granted he was topless and in a wheelchair with nowhere to run to, but Bettie didn't want him to feel embarrassed. Weren't meeting the parents meant to be great?

Bettie frowned as she realised how stupid that was. Meeting Graham's parents was not grand, it had been flat out traumatic more than anything else.

Then a tall elegant woman walked up to Harry's father's side and wrapped her thin arms around his.

She was probably five, ten years younger than him and her skin was cloud-white and her thin face didn't show a single pore. Bettie wondered if she was a model, or at least a former model.

She looked that good.

Especially as the woman wore a long black dress, a golden necklace and even from two metres away Bettie could smell her expensive flowery perfume.

"Get. Away!" Harry's father shouted.

Bettie saw that Graham was about to step forward and probably pull the detective card, but Bettie didn't see the need just yet. Harry's father was angry but Bettie would definitely be if she had heard her children were in hospital.

Bettie stepped in front of everyone. "Mr..."

"Rafael Rossi," Harry's father said.

Bettie bowed slightly. She had no idea why.

"We all want the same thing here," Bettie said, "both of our loved ones were attacked tonight. We need to find out what happened,"

Mr Rossi laughed. "Where the cops? Where the two I saw coming out? Why was your bambino be okay?"

Bettie realised Mr Rossi must have left school before English was the normal in schools, but she knew plenty of English people who couldn't speak English as good as him.

Bettie heard Sean open his mouth, but she waved him silent.

"I hear you're English," Bettie said looking at the

woman.

"Yes, I'm Miss Bella Rossi,"

"A very pretty name," Bettie said. "Can we all agree to get along so we can find out what happened to our young people?"

Bella looked at Mr Rossi with a smile, but he shook his head, and started talking in a very fast Italian.

Thankfully Bettie had had an Italian boyfriend years ago so she knew a bit, but Sean shot up and started shouting back in Italian.

Rather perfect Italian actually. Bettie was really impressed.

From what Bettie could understand it was something about Mr Rossi told Bella something like this was going to happen and they shouldn't have shipped Harry off to the UK to get an education and explore his sexuality. He believed they should have… sent him to the Monks and they would cure him of the demonic influence.

Now Bettie couldn't care less about religion and thankfully as much as the Political leaders of England banged on about their religious beliefs, the UK as a whole wasn't very religious (unless you included Northern Ireland). But Italy from what she understood was a very different story, Bettie felt sorry for Harry.

Sean started waving his hand at Mr Rossi and really shouted at him.

Graham just looked at Bettie. "What he's

saying?"

"Something about Sean loves Harry more than he ever did," Bettie said. "Now Sean saying how great Harry is and never talk about Harry that way again,"

Bettie smiled.

"What?" Graham asked.

"He's speaking more passionately about Harry to Mr Rossi than you ever spoke to your mother about me," Bettie said.

Graham frowned. "I…"

Bettie smiled. "It's okay. I promise,"

Bettie didn't think that was true but they all had more pressing matters at the moment.

"Excuse me!" Nurse Lucas shouted who were still standing there.

Everyone went silent.

Bettie looked at Lucas. "Please. Tell us all,"

"I am his father! You will tell me and my wife. You will not tell these… people,"

Sean's face went pale then Bettie gasped as she saw Sean's bandages were now wet with blood.

Sean collapsed into the wheelchair.

"Nurse!" Lucas shouted.

A female nurse popped out of Harry's hospital room and took Sean away to be stitched back up.

"I'll go with him," Graham said, following them.

Bettie ran after him quickly and pulled him closer.

"Get me pictures of his stab wounds for Zoey," Bettie said.

Graham gave her a firm nod. If anyone could identify what weapon could have stabbed Sean, it would definitely be Senior Forensic Specialist Zoey Quill.

Bettie wasn't impressed with Mr Rossi, she hated to think about all the rage he had caused Sean and now something bad might happen to him all because this man didn't like Sean. That was outrageous. And whatever smart thinking Sean had done earlier in the evening (like wrapping his belt around himself to slow down his bleeding) had now failed.

Sean's fate was now in the hands of others. Again. And that terrified Bettie.

Bettie could only frown as she stared at Mr Rossi who was smiling at her. He really wasn't a fan of her, then Nurse Lucas looked at her.

"I'm sorry Miss English. The doctor will only allow family into the hospital room," he said.

Bettie rolled her eyes at him as he lead them into the room to see their son. She couldn't help but feel so powerless to help Harry.

The cops were never going to help a foreign gay man, and the chance of Graham being allowed to investigate was slim to none.

So Bettie smiled as she realised she was going to have to investigate this by herself and hoping she could find some evidence of criminal activity that would allow Graham to get involved.

Thankfully (Bettie wasn't sure if that was the correct term) Sean had been stabbed. That meant someone was carrying an offensive weapon about Canterbury, so maybe, just maybe that was the argument Graham could use.

A few seconds later Nurse Lucas came out of the hospital room smiling, smiling and he pulled Bettie to one side.

"You're the private eye, right?" he asked.

Bettie smiled and nodded.

"And you're investigating this? And everything I say won't come back to me," Lucas asked.

"Of course not," Bettie said, firmly.

Lucas nodded. "Then I'm off shift now and I suggest you buy me something in the canteen,"

Bettie grinned at him. "Why?"

Lucas started to walk down the corridor. "Because I'm going to tell you what the Doctor's report said. I looked at it. But prepare yourself. It's bad,"

Bettie felt her stomach tighten and now she wasn't sure she actually wanted to know.

CHAPTER 4
16th June 2022
Canterbury, England

Graham was completely surprised at how awkward he felt as both a cop and a boyfriend right now.

As Graham stood in one corner whilst a tall, very beautiful female nurse helped Sean onto the hospital bed, he had to admit that Graham really hated hospitals. They were simply awful places that smelt of horrid lemony, orange and clove scented chemicals that only hide the underlying smell of death and decay.

Graham flat out hated hospitals.

As the nurse got Sean who was still topless and just wearing some black jogging bottoms to keep his legs warm, Graham couldn't feel any more sorry for him. Graham could see the pain Sean was in and that was probably just from the emotional torture of knowing someone you loved was injured.

Then Graham heard the nurse hiss as she looked at all the blood soaking Sean's bandages were looked to tightly wrapped around him. But as terrible as that was, Graham was a little bit impressed.

It was almost refreshing to Graham seeing someone defend the person they loved and standing up for them even at personal risk. Sean could have stayed quiet whilst Harry's parents moaned about both men, but he didn't. He made sure he defended Harry, even if it would make Harry's parents hate him forever.

That was inspiring.

Then Graham realised the only reason it was so inspiring was because he wished he had the balls to do it with his own parents. He loved Bettie more than anything else in the world and he would always, always defend her.

Unless it was in front of his mother.

And Graham knew that was a terrible, cowardice thing to do, but he couldn't help himself. He didn't want to be rude to his mother, but then why was it okay for her to be racist, homophobic and an utter bitch to Bettie and other people?

It made no sense, and first thing tomorrow Graham was going to tell his mother that, and in all honesty, Graham didn't need her. He had Bettie and her wonderful family, so if his mother really hated him and his choices that much.

Then so be it!

Sean hissing made Graham frown as he watched

Sean bite his lip as the nurse unwrapped his bandages and revealed the bloody wound. Graham had no idea where the wound started and stopped, there was so much blood.

And knowing that he had to take pictures so Zoey could give them a weapon, it just felt so weird.

As a cop Graham knew the importance of taking pictures and giving them to the crime lab so they could find a match. But as a person and Bettie's boyfriend, it felt so weird taking pictures of a man's bare stomach and considering Sean was old enough to be his extremely young brother, or child if Graham had had children when he was 16.

It just didn't feel right.

But as Graham watched the nurse gently wipe away the blood, he realised he just had to focus and make sure he caught the people who did this. Because absolutely no one threatened his family and got away with it.

No matter what the other cops said.

"Excuse me Nurse," Graham quietly said.

"Yes Detective," the nurse said.

"I need… I need to take some pictures of the wound to send to a Forensic Specialist. May I?"

The nurse frowned then slowly exchanged glances between Graham and the door. After a few moments the nurse closed the door.

"I know you aren't officially investigating Detective. I could lose my job over this," the Nurse said, picking up a sealed pack of bandages.

Graham gestured he was sorry.

"But," the Nurse said, dropping the pack, "if I need to find something on the floor. Then I can't see what you're doing and cannot protest,"

The Nurse knelt down on the floor and pretended to look for the pack of bandages.

Graham whipped out his phone and gestured Sean to lean back so he could see the stab wound clearly.

Now the nurse had cleaned it perfectly, Graham was really disgusted at the beasts that attacked Sean and Harry. Thankfully because Sean was really fit, there was no fatty tissues that blocked or created shadows obscuring the wound.

From what Graham could understand, the stab wound was fairly deep (judging by the colour of the blood dripping out) and judging by the almost invisible stitching done to the wound. It was at least five centimetres wide.

A massive blade did this. This was more like a meat-carving knife than a knife for cutting vegetables.

Someone wanted to kill here.

"Glad I wrapped my belt round it," Sean said hissing in pain.

Graham nodded.

During all the chaos, he had been carrying Harry and focusing on him whilst Bettie focused on Sean. And he remembered Bettie muttering something about a belt being tied round Sean when she found him.

Graham was just glad he was okay.

The nurse shot up. "I must treat him now,"

Sean fell onto the bed and his face was almost ghostly white.

The nurse just looked at Graham and Graham left.

As he walked back down the corridor, he felt his stomach tighten into an extremely painful knot as he heard an alarm go and doctors and nurses rushed in.

Whatever happened Sean had lost a hell of a lot of blood.

Graham just hoped (prayed more likely), it wasn't too much.

Graham had to find out who did this.

Regardless of whether Sean made it or not.

CHAPTER 5
17th June 2022
Canterbury, England

With it now past midnight, Bettie was rather (and very pleasantly) surprised to see how empty the massive hospital canteen was with its long rows upon rows of metal tables and chairs, a long buffet counter that was now closed and an unlimited tea and coffee machine was open.

If Bettie wasn't pregnant then maybe she would have been extremely pleased, but she was and she was much more concerned about her nephew at the moment.

But she had to admit as she watched Nurse Lucas making himself a cup of hot chocolate with vegan milk (he fully understood Bettie's pregnant body's needs), she had to admit he was very different from what she had been expecting.

It was extremely clear as they walked down to the canteen that he was gay and that he truly loved his job as a nurse. It had taken them half an hour to do a five-minute walk because even though he was off shift, he was making sure other patients and staff were okay and if there was a stranger walking the corridor looking lost then he would help them.

He wasn't getting paid for helping those people. Yet he did it anyway.

To Bettie that was just flat out amazing, and considering he was helping her out, the least she could

do was buy him a drink. Because apparently giving him £10 was far too much for him only doing his job.

And now Bettie understood what she sounded like to other people.

When he sat back down opposite her, he smiled and took a sip of amazing looking coffee.

"Thanks for doing this," Bettie said, quietly.

"It's fine," Lucas said, "I'm technically a doctor now. Finished school and exams last month. Just waiting for the paperwork to go through the hospital so shouldn't get into as much trouble yet for theoretically telling you this,"

Bettie smiled. She loved a person who was willing to bend the rules to help her do the right thing. It was just a shame how many doctors she had seen fired or suspended for a week or two, because they had wanted to help Private Eyes do the right thing.

She was NOT going to let that happen to Lucas.

"Bettie!" someone shouted.

Bettie looked around and shot up when she saw a woman wearing a blue dressing grown that made her look over 60 with her messy hair, awful bags under her eyes and her untidiness.

Bettie had no idea her sister Phryne had been sleeping when she called about Sean and Harry.

Phryne grabbed her tight. "Where's my son! Where's my son!"

Bettie couldn't force the words out.

"Where is he! Where's my son!"

Phryne was screaming as loud as she could. Bettie looked at Lucas. She couldn't form the words in her mouth, she couldn't say what had happened to Sean again.

Just calling her sister and telling her, her son was in critical condition had been awful enough.

"Julie," Lucas said.

Bettie watched a very young student nurse walk over and Bettie wondered if she was technically on her coffee break.

Lucas came over and slowly took Phryne off Bettie.

"Julie. Please take this woman to room 501. The stabbing victim," Lucas said.

"Oh god! Oh god!" Phryne shouted as loud as she could.

Lucas gently hugged Phryne and passed her over to Julie.

"Miss," Lucas said, "this is nurse Julie. She's

going to take you to your son. Is that okay?"

Phryne started screaming and crying at the same time. Then Lucas simply nodded to Julie to start taking (dragging) her to Sean's room.

Bettie just stared at Phryne for a few moments and rubbed her baby bump. She couldn't know what her sister was going through at the moment, but she knew one day she could have to. And it really, really scared her.

She had been tempted to ask where Sean's dad, John, was but she knew the answer. He was always bloody working making sure that the stars, celebrities or whoever he worked with had everything they needed. Bettie realised that he had been in Los Angeles recently helping the producer of a new film keep one of the more temperamental stars happy.

Bettie was hopeful that John was now on a plane back here. His son needed him after all. But the last thing Bettie was going to do was depend on John for help.

Bettie and Lucas sat back down at the table.

"Thanks," Bettie said. "I… you're amazing,"

Lucas smiled. "We don't get a lot of… um, people with those injuries but I try my best to comfort families. How are you doing?"

Bettie didn't know how to answer such a thing. She loved Sean and Harry so much, but just the idea of what happened was too much to bear.

"I don't know. Please, you must have to get home. What did you see on Harry's report?" Bettie said.

Lucas gently took Bettie's hand and rubbed it. she didn't know how many hospital rules he was breaking, but she felt perfectly safe and it was comforting.

"My husband's," Lucas said, "a fireman working nights. I have all night. But I wasn't kidding when I said Harry's report wasn't good,"

Bettie frowned as she saw a canteen staff member walk over to the tea and coffee machine and presumably refill it.

"Theoretically and of course, this is simply a guess," Lucas said, loud enough that the staff member heard.

Bettie smiled.

"Harry is in," Lucas said, quietly, "a medically induced coma. The bruising is already starting to show and it's only been a few hours. Normally, the worse of the bruising would come out tomorrow. It's come out now,"

Bettie gently rubbed her baby bump.

"The doctors think he was beaten probably within an inch of his life. His nose was broken. There were x-rays and there are multiple bones broken and…"

Bettie frowned. She hated when medical staff just trailed off like that.

"What?" Bettie asked.

"There is considerable evidence," Lucas said, "that Harry's brain's swelling. Hence the induced coma,"

Bettie wanted to be sick.

"We won't know the effects of the brain swelling until it's stopped and we release him from the coma. Then we'll send him to neurology, the brain people, and they can see what's happening,"

Bettie really, really wanted to be sick.

"What… give me best and worst outcome," Bettie said slowly.

Lucas finished off his hot chocolate. "I think… and please know I am *not* a neurologist. I think he could just have minor brain damage that could heal over time. Like a stutter, poor coordination or balance. To… the much more extreme effects of him developing more severe symptoms,"

Bettie just waved her hands to be silent. She had read more than enough academic articles in her life to understand the effects of brain injuries. Some people developed permeant memory problems. Like people who couldn't remember what they did five minutes ago, and other people could remember what they did ten minutes ago, but not a year ago.

Other people could make massive life decisions but it was impossible for them to get dress.

And worse of all (in Bettie's opinion) was people with concussions and other brain injuries were more likely to get dementia in later life.

Bettie of course knew that these things were much more complicated than a brain injury, but they all tended to stem from the injury. Bettie just hoped that Harry would be okay.

But there was something even worse that concerned Bettie.

How the hell was she meant to tell Sean.

How the hell was she meant to tell him the man he loved might not be the same man when he woke up.

Bettie just didn't know.

She didn't have a clue.

CHAPTER 6
17th June 2022
Canterbury, England

Graham was rather shocked at how this case was affecting him. As a cop he had seen plenty of violent crimes over the past two decades and they had actually made him sleep better (probably because he just wanted to forget them), but after getting in and putting Bettie to sleep on the sofa at 2 pm. Graham had struggled to get much sleep.

At best he only had six hours.

But after two hours of trying to get back to sleep, Graham had decided that if he wasn't going to forget the case in dreamland. He might have let Bettie sleep and he should work.

As Graham just watched Bettie snorting away on the large black sofa pressed against the wall of their massive living room, he was really pleased to see her sound asleep and resting herself and the babies.

Graham loved the wonderful warmth from the

coffee mug in his hands and that made the utterly amazing smells of coffee, oat milk and lots of golden syrup (more sweetness than sugar) fill his senses.

Graham forced himself to look away from Bettie who was so cute when she slept, but he wasn't a fan of the snorting. And Graham focused on the three massive whiteboards he had put up this morning around the living room.

Considering their living room was easily twenty metres long and another ten high (Bettie made tons of money hence the nice house), Graham was surprised how large the whiteboards were. There was barely enough space to swing a cat in here.

As annoyed (and furious) Graham was about the attack, he knew that the only way to help Sean and Harry was to find the monsters that did this, and hopefully find something that would force the police to open an official investigation.

Otherwise Graham was going to have to use a trick that he hated. He was going to have to leak the attack to the media and then drag the police into public shaming. All because a few senior officers didn't care about two young men being almost killed.

As Graham focused on the whiteboards he realised that they barely knew anything about the case. The second and third whiteboards were completely blank, that was where Graham was hoping to add suspects and evidence as they found it.

So far they had none.

Yet on the first whiteboard, Graham had stuck a

few pictures of Sean and Harry, their ties at the university and Sean's stab wound.

He had had a voicemail from Phryne earlier and Graham really wasn't looking forward to telling Bettie was had happened over night, and the status report on both men. They still didn't know about Harry because his idiot of a father wasn't allowing Phryne in to see him.

But it turned out the reason why Sean had collapsed last night was because of something called Hypovolemic shock, since Sean had lost so much blood his heart didn't have enough blood to pump round his body.

Graham hated that that had happened to Sean.

But Graham seriously hated that apparently Sean had woke up in the night screaming, ripped out his IV drip and sliced his arm on the edge.

From what Phryne said it wasn't a suicide attempt, it was just how reckless and panicked Sean had ripped out his IV because he thought he was in danger.

Even if that was the case, Graham was not going to let Sean feel the need to end himself. All because he might feel like Harry (the love of his life) was gone.

As soon as Bettie (and the twins) were up and okay, Graham was going straight back to the hospital and he was going to use, and probably abuse, whatever police power he could to make sure he saw Harry.

Not only so Graham could see for himself the damage and his injuries, but just to make sure he could tell Sean how the man he loved was.

Yet that was the odd thing about the entire case, Graham might not have been able to interview Sean or Harry last night (and sadly might not be able to for a while). But from what he understood there was literally no reason to attack them.

Graham had seriously deep dived into Harry's life before he started university in England and during his time at university. There was nothing of note. He wasn't a part of any political clubs, no strange clubs or anything that could even make him a target.

Same went for Sean.

All their friends, lectures and everyone they encountered said how wonderful Sean and Harry were.

Leaving Graham to really wonder if the reason for the attack was the most obvious. Had they been attacked for the sole reason they were gay?

Graham knew England was probably the worse place for gays in the United Kingdom (after Northern Ireland) because large parts of the country were still deeply religious even if they didn't go to church. And even the people who didn't go to church, still believe it was weird, unnatural and it shouldn't happen.

Graham smiled at that. It was amazing how a few thousand years of religions teaching that gays are unholy abominations could just get so engrained into a culture that people just believed it without knowing why.

Graham went over to the first whiteboard and simply wrote *gay?* As a possible motive for the attack, but he still felt as if there was something more to this.

Thankfully, he had managed to call Zoey Quill this morning and she had agreed to look through the photos of Sean's stab wound and attempt to give them a possible weapon.

Graham wasn't too hopeful but just the fact that Zoey wanted to try was more than he had expected.

Bettie's phone started to buzz. Bettie snorted louder.

As much as Graham didn't like looking at her phone, given the situation, he felt like he had to.

Graham looked at her phone and cocked his head. It was a text message from Phryne saying Sean was waking, alert and only wanted to talk to her.

"That's my phone," Bettie said, taking it out his hand and reading the message.

"Sorry-"

Bettie waved him silent. "It's fine babe. I would have done the same. Give me… ten minutes. Change of clothes and we'll go,"

Graham folded his arms and frowned.

"What?" Bettie asked.

Graham just pointed to her baby bump. He wasn't having either one of them putting themselves or their babies' health ahead of this case.

Regardless of how personal it was.

"Eat. Drink. Then we go," Graham said firmly.

Bettie smiled and nodded and then kissed Graham.

"You're going to be an amazing dad," Bettie said walking towards the kitchen.

Graham really did love that amazing woman.

CHAPTER 7
17th June 2022
Canterbury, England

Bettie was really impressed with Graham's take-charge attitude the second he walked into the hospital. And thankfully they were finally going to get somewhere with seeing Harry and knowing the type of injuries he had sustained.

So whilst Graham was off doing that Bettie was more than determined to talk to Sean, which because of Phryne's text, Bettie was rather concerned about.

It also didn't help that Graham hadn't waited fifteen minutes after she woke up to tell her about Sean screaming in the middle of the night. Bettie just wanted him to be okay.

Bettie didn't even want to imagine how impossible this was for him. Bettie utterly hated the idea of anything happening to Graham and it almost killed her when she thought of him as in danger.

So if Graham was actually in a coma in a hospital

and Bettie couldn't see him... she honestly had no clue how she would cope.

Bettie stood over Sean's blue hospital bed with the horrible life sign machines beeping away and an IV line connected into his left arm. But the more alarming thing was Sean's right arm had been restrained and quite literally handcuffed to the bed railings.

And it concerned her a lot how poorly and ill Sean looked, his skin was still ghostly white, he was far from the beautiful, healthy man she had seen last night right after the stabbing.

Bettie had to solve this.

Sean slowly moved his restrained hand and gestured that he wanted her to hold it. she did. For some reason Sean's hand seeing perfectly warm shocked her.

"How you feel?" Bettie asked.

Sean smiled. "Like I got a knife rammed through me,"

Bettie didn't smile. "Why the restraint? And why you want to talk to only me?"

Sean hissed slightly. "I panicked last night. Jumped after a nightmare, you came in here and told me Harry was dead. I woke up, jumped and ripped out my IV line,"

Bettie gently rubbed his hand.

"Sliced my arm accidentally. Nurses thought I tried to... end my pain,"

Bettie kissed him on the head.

"I know you're investigating," Sean said.

Bettie nodded. "Tell me. What happened?"

Sean frowned and closed his eyes.

"Me and Harry both had exams yesterday. Our last ones ever. We were going out to celebrate just the two of us, we going to some clubs, then an after-party for final years,"

Bettie took a few breaths of the chemically-scented air.

"Then later we were going to come back to ours and... you know. Celebrate like couples do," Sean said.

"Why didn't you two go out with friends?" Bettie asked.

Sean opened his eyes and weakly smiled. "They wanted to go to clubs in the afternoon. Do a lot of day drinking and some wanted to do drugs. Me and Harry don't do either of them, so we spent the afternoon walking out about, shopping and talking. It was rather wonderful,"

Bettie realised she really had to do more of that with Graham.

"What happened in the evening?" Bettie asked.

Sean gave Bettie a real schoolboy smile.

"Harry treated me to a posh dinner. He surprised me by taking me to this great French place off the high street. I said it was too much, but he said I had worked so hard for the past three years I was worth it,"

Bettie felt her stomach twist. She really didn't

want to tell him Harry was in a coma and probably had a brain injury.

"We were walking back from the restaurant. Our friends were at a club and were waiting for us before we went to the after-party. We walked through the…"

Bettie held Sean's hand tight as his eyes widened and sweat started to pour back his face.

"You're safe," Bettie said. "I'm here,"

"We were walking through the castle-like tunnel into the high street. Three men jumped us. All black. They went for Harry. I couldn't let him get hurt. I felt the knife. The knife!"

Bettie hugged Sean.

"I was kicked in the head after. I fell to the ground. One had a pipe. He whacked Harry. Again and again and again. I screamed. He didn't make a sound. A homeless man came out,"

Bettie bit her lip. No one should ever have to go through that.

"The three men ran away. I got up and picked up Harry. I had to find someone. I had to find you. I… The knife!"

Sean screamed and screamed and screamed.

Sean gripped onto Bettie's wrist.

He was hurting her.

Bettie pulled away.

Sean scratched her.

Bettie rushed to the door.

"Nurse!" Bettie shouted.

Second later nurses rushed in and sedated Sean,

he kept screaming and shouting for Harry until the drugs finally kicked in and forced him to go to sleep.

Bettie grabbed her arm. She knew Sean didn't mean to hurt her, but he was clearly traumatised by the attack and she had no doubt that Sean had watched Harry basically die (as far as Sean was concerned he probably was).

As Bettie left the hospital room, it became clear to her that no matter what, these three men were going to pay for what they did.

Now whether they paid legally or not.

That didn't matter to Bettie.

No one attacked, traumatised and stabbed her family without some kind of vengeance.

Bettie was now firmly on a war path.

CHAPTER 8
17th June 2022
Canterbury, England

Thankfully when Graham went into Harry's large white hospital room there was only him, Harry and Bella in there. Before now, Graham hadn't known how pleased he was that Harry's father wasn't in there.

Graham smiled at Bella who was wearing a wonderful yellow summer dress, white trainers and playing on her phone. She waved Graham in and he was really pleased that she wasn't arguing or shouting at him.

But the closer Graham got to Harry's large metal hospital bed, the sadder he felt.

Harry had always been an extremely healthy young man with olive-coloured skin, a slightly muscular body and a very handsome face. And even though Graham had never looked at another man, he could at least remotely understand why Sean found him attractive.

But if Graham didn't know what Harry looked like before. He would have no idea what Harry was like before the attack.

Harry's face was transformed with bandages and a massive ventilation tube had been forced down his throat, so he could breathe whilst in his coma.

Yet all of Harry's arms, legs and chest were covered in plaster and metal stints were in place to help all the bones heal themselves.

This was horrific.

"We both love him you know," Bella said.

Graham could only nod. He was too shocked about Harry. He was such a great, wonderful man who never ever deserved this. And the harsh lemony smell from the cleaning chemicals only added to Graham's discomfort.

"And that is why Mr Rossi the police will not investigate," a familiar man said.

Graham turned out and his hands formed fists when he saw Mr Rossi walk in with a tall man worn in a fine tight suit, black shoes and holding an expensive pocket watch.

Officer Caleb Young was an utter dickhead as far as Graham was concerned, and clearly he had been doing great in pursuing and ass-licking the older, senior police cops.

Graham hated Caleb because he was the most homophobic cop he had ever met. Caleb had even forced a gay schoolboy to be stripped searched. There was no reason, but Caleb had *wanted to teach the little F*g a lesson.*

It took everything Graham had not to beat the life out of Caleb right there and then. How dare this fucking idiot stop the police investigating what happened to his nephew.

Graham wanted to kill him!

"Detective Adams," Caleb said with a smile, "I'm hardly surprised you're hanging round these scum and unholy creatures,"

Graham was utterly shocked. Before Caleb had at least tried to try his hatred for gays, but he clearly believed he was so protected in the police that he was untouchable.

"Officer Young," Graham said bitterly.

"Actually. It is Detective Sergeant Young now,"

Graham laughed.

"You know you really should try to cozy up to the senior officers. You can get anything if you play by the rules," Caleb said.

"The racist, homophobic and sexist rules you mean," Graham said.

Caleb simply smiled. "I'll give you a choice Detective. As your superior officer, I will give you the weekend to investigate the case. On Monday, you come into work and behave like the good cop you are,"

Graham wanted to swear at him so badly.

"You're giving me a day and an afternoon to solve a crime," Graham said.

"There is no crime here Graham. I don't believe trying to get rid of gays is a crime. It was always a mistake to make their disease illegal,"

Caleb simply walked away and Graham looked at Mr Rossi who was swearing in very fast Italian.

"Mr Rossi," Graham said carefully, "I promise you not all British cops are like that,"

Mr Rossi frowned. "But the cops in charge are like that. Am I wrong?"

Graham wanted to so badly to tell him otherwise, but he couldn't. If these people did become family through a marriage in the future, Graham hardly wanted to start their relationship with a lie.

No matter how badly he wanted to tell it.

"Investigate!" Mr Rossi shouted.

Bella went over to her husband and hugged him.

"Detective," she said, "do whatever it takes. We're hiring you and your girlfriend. We'll pay whatever it takes. Just fine the bastards that did this to our son and…"

Bella looked at Mr Rossi.

Rafael Rossi smiled. "And fine out who did this to our Sean,"

Graham didn't know why. But that made him smile.

Raefel hugged Graham. "In Italy, we're huggers Detective,"

"Call me Graham," he said.

Rafael nodded. "I don't hate your Sean. He's a great kid and I was… just angry earlier. In Italy…"

Rafael started to suggest to his wife, almost like he couldn't find the English to explain it properly.

Bella nodded. "We live in Roma. Just outside Vatican City actually, so you can imagine it. We see the pope and our neighbourhood lives and breathes Catholicism, and a month before Harry left for uni. A gay man was tortured and executed by some catholic purists. Harry was terrified,"

Graham could imagine.

"Harry came out to us. But we were scared for him, we screamed, shouted and threw stuff at him. We were vile until the day he left. But we love him so damn much," Bella said.

As much as Graham wanted to moan at them, he could see in their eyes how awful they felt about abandoning and being so vile to their son. And whilst it wasn't what Graham would do in the same situation, he could just about understand it.

Bella and Rafael were just trying to protect their son at the end of the day.

And now they were in a hospital room with their son in a coma, Graham would hate to imagine how awful they felt. For as far as they knew, their son might die thinking his parents thought of him as an abomination.

Bettie knocked at the door. "I don't charge family,"

Graham smiled and kissed her on the head. She was great at hiding behind doors and listening.

Rafael kissed her and Bella hugged her. Then

Bettie looked at Graham.

"We have a case to solve," Bettie said. "Take pictures of the wounds and we need to go to Zoey's,"

"Definitely," Graham said. "We certainly have a case most personal,"

CHAPTER 9
17ᵗʰ June 2022
Canterbury, England

Bettie was quickly beginning to realise how little she nor Graham actually knew about Senior Forensic Specialist Zoey Quill's private life.

Zoey had been such an amazing help to Graham over the decades on the various cases, and Bettie had gotten to know her fairly well over her more recent cases. Like investigating Russians two months ago and then later trying to track down a bunch of stolen computer equipment.

Zoey was amazing.

But as Bettie and Graham waited patiently in Zoey's massive bedroom with a perfectly made queen-size bed with blue silk sheets, breath-taking art and tons of fancy jewellery on various cabinets. Bettie was really realising she had no clue about Zoey's private life.

Even the constant sound of little children

running around downstairs with screaming, laughing and (some attempts at) talking echoed all around the bedroom. Bettie was seriously looking forward to that in a year or two.

But judging by Graham's face, he also had no idea Zoey was a mother or that her husband (or wife?) had such a good job.

And even the bedroom smelt wonderful with hints of orange, cloves and almonds filling the air in some strange combination that seriously worked. Bettie needed to find out what Zoey used.

A few moments later the bedroom opened and Zoey shook Graham's hands and hugged Bettie. Bettie had to admit she looked good for a Saturday with her bright blue shorts, t-shirt and bright pink painted toenails.

"I'm so sorry about this Zoe," Graham said.

Zoey mockingly hit him. "Don't be stupid. If someone attacks Sean or you two, someone attacks my kids!"

It was great to know Zoey liked them that much, Bettie needed to remember that.

"Did you look at the photos we sent?" Bettie asked.

Zoey nodded. "Yea, the knife wound from Sean and then the pictures of Harry, right?"

Bettie nodded.

"I won't lie Graham," Zoey said, "but your picture taking abilities need serious work. And I mean serious,"

"Told you," Bettie said.

Graham carefully elbowed her in the ribs.

"Even with awful pictures, I can almost certainly say you are looking for a blade that is 2 inches wide. Certainly a knife used for cutting meat or hunting," Zoey said.

That really didn't make Bettie feel any better. These three men were savages enough, she didn't really want to know about a massive knife.

"And the depth is probably," Zoey said, "ten centimetres perhaps. It definitely cut deep judging by the colour of the blood. Sean's luckily to be alive,"

"Still suffered hypovolemic shock," Graham said.

Zoey frowned. "I can confirm Harry was almost probably hit with a pipe. And judging by the damage, it would have to be a metal pipe, and maybe a small pipe,"

"Can you give us a rough size?" Bettie asked.

Little hands started tapping on the bedroom door.

"Ma! Ma! Ma!" a little voice shouted.

Zoey laughed and went over to the door.

"What is it angel face?" she said.

"George isn't letting me play. It's my toy," the little girl said.

Zoey tapped her on the nose which made her laugh.

"Are you taking in turns?" she said in a baby-like voice.

The little girl looked at the floor.

"Nora," Zoey said, "what did we say about sharing?"

"We need to,"

"And what happens when we don't share?" Zoey said smiling.

"The trolls take our toys at night,"

Zoey kissed her on the head. "Share with your brother. Mummy will be downstairs in a minute,"

"Okay ma. Looove you,"

"Love you too sweetheart," Zoey said watching her daughter walk down the stairs and she closed the door.

Bettie was really impressed. She had to meet up with Zoey before the baby came to learn some tips.

"Call me any time Bet," Zoey said.

Bettie smiled. She didn't realise her shock was so visible.

"Right," Zoey said. "The pipe. I would say the pipe was big and heavy enough for a person to have to swing with two hands. But not so heavy that the momentum would cause him to be thrown with the pipe,"

That meant almost nothing to Bettie.

Zoey smiled. "Um, think less water pipes for your house and more pumping pipes about the size of a 2 by 4 piece of wood,"

Now Bettie understood.

"Thanks Zoe," Graham said, and all three of them started to go downstairs.

Zoey went down first so she could get back to

playing with her kids sooner. Bettie loved that.

Graham went close to Bettie's ear. "Not calling our son George,"

"Definitely not," Bettie whispered. "Don't like Nora either,"

"Thank god," Graham said.

Bettie and Graham went out the front door.

"So two names down," Bettie said smiling, "thousands more to go,"

CHAPTER 10
17th June 2022
Canterbury, England

Graham was still furious about that idiot Caleb Young getting promoted ahead of him. After all Graham was the good cop who wanted to help, protect and support victims of crime. But no, that clearly wasn't how the police worked and Graham knew that.

He wanted to change it, but that was a damn near impossible task.

What Graham loved about Canterbury high street was even though it was a wonderfully warm and sunny Saturday late afternoon, there was such a great atmosphere with students walking up and down the cobblestone street whilst they shopped, talked and listened to the musicians playing in the street.

Young families were great seeing the sites and going out for an amazing meal, and that was what Graham loved about the high street. It was a place that just came alive and was perfect for all ages.

But Graham and Bettie were here for a recent so Graham turned away from the cobblestone high street and focused on the entrance to the street that made people walk under a massive castle turret with two openings to walk through.

The first was designed like a massive castle gate with the gate taken out, it was probably inspired by the Roman occupation of Canterbury thousands of years ago.

That entrance would be awful for an attack because it was far too open and it was mainly designed for vehicles to drive through.

Yet the second entrance involved a footpath that was a lot more sheltered from sight and it made people walk through a little arch with beautiful high stone walls. That was why tons of homeless people slept in there at night, it definitely beat the wet and cold street.

Normally it was very light and it really added to the historic atmosphere of canterbury, but at night it was almost pitch black. Especially with the streetlight not working.

Graham and Bettie went over to the second entrance and Graham just had to smile at the impressiveness of the archway. He felt like he was walking through a portal into history, it was made that well. It felt as if he actually was in Roman times with the city wall and other castles.

Graham nodded at the two homeless men who

were sitting there trying to cool themselves down.

"We're looking for any signs of blood," Bettie said.

Graham nodded. He looked down at the stone ground of the archway but it was so wet and dirty he doubted they would find too much.

As Graham kept looking at the dirty ground, he wondered if this was the right time to talk about their other little problem about the naming.

"I'll tell you Bet," Graham said, "we aren't calling our children Serenity or Caleb,"

Bettie laughed. Graham really hated the name Serenity as that was the awful name of Caleb's equally homophobic girlfriend.

Graham hated both of them.

"Got nothing," Graham said.

Bettie looked at him. "There's nothing here too,"

Graham looked at the two homeless men. Both of them looked rather youngish, maybe 35, and compared to some people who faked homelessness, these two really were homeless. Graham had never seen two people look so ill and unhealthy.

Graham took out two ten pound notes. "We're looking for something. If I give you two this money, can we ask you two to move please? Only for a few minutes?"

Each man nodded and looked as if they wanted to say something but Graham could only hear murmurs through their cracked lips.

Graham gave them the money and the two men

quickly moved for them.

"Thank you," Bettie said.

But sadly Graham could only see more dirt, grim and rubbish on the ground. This wasn't getting them anywhere, but at least he had helped two people.

Bettie went over to the two homeless men. "How long have you two been here?"

The men looked at each other nervously. "Cops?"

Graham smiled. "I'm not going to do anything,"

Both men slowly nodded. "Last night,"

Graham smiled. That was great news.

"Did you two see anything? Like two young men walking through here. One had blond hair with pink highlights," Bettie asked.

One of the men really smiled. "Yea. He was hot,"

Bettie laughed. "Thank you. He's my nephew. Did you see anything happen to them?"

Both men looked at Graham carefully and gestured Bettie to get closer.

Graham couldn't hear what they were saying but he didn't like it. Considering at least one of these people were homeless probably because they were gay. Graham couldn't deny he was concerned about their attitudes towards the police.

Bettie took a few steps back. "He won't hurt you,"

Graham felt his stomach twist.

"We got some dinner. Saved all month for a fast food dinner," one of the men said.

"Yea," the other man said. "We were coming back here for the night. We saw your hot nephew and his friend. They were laughing, having a great time. Three men ran at them,"

Graham held Bettie's hands tight.

"Two men were dressed in black. One was holding a knife, another a pipe. They run at your hottie's friend. Your nephew jumped in front of them, they stabbed him again,"

Graham nodded slowly. It was so hard listening to this. Then he realised something.

"Wait you said three men in black?" Graham asked.

The homeless men shook their heads. "No. Two men dressed in black. Third man, very dark blue and he was wearing…"

Both homeless men looked at the ground.

Bettie knelt down. Graham helped her down.

"You can trust us," she said.

"He was wearing a cop logo. Something about a cop bar near here," they both said at the same time.

Graham wanted to be sick.

"You two!" Caleb Young shouted.

Graham felt furious as he saw Caleb in his suit and two uniformed officers walk up to the homeless men, and the uniforms arrested them.

"What are you doing!" Graham shouted.

"Homelessness and begging is illegal under UK law," Caleb said, "I am simply following the law to the letter. Something a lot of cops should be doing, this country would be a hell of a lot better off if they did that,"

Then as the uniformed officers took the homeless men away, Caleb just smiled.

"And you heard it yourself," he said, "one of them is a degenerate. We cannot allow these unholy people to keep spreading their infection through our society,"

As Graham watched Caleb walk away, he felt his stomach tighten into an extremely painful knot. This wasn't right. It wasn't fair. It wasn't justice.

This had to stop.

Then Graham's eyes slid down for some reason to Caleb's trousers and he gasped.

Right on the left ass-cheek was a logo of a very local cop bar.

The *Cop and Justice Bar* just off the high street.

Fear gripped Graham.

The idea of Caleb attacking Harry and Sean terrified him more than he ever wanted to admit.

CHAPTER 11
17th June 2022
Canterbury, England

Bettie just held Graham as they both sat on their large sofa in their living room surrounded by the three massive whiteboards as Graham just shook his head.

This must have been torture plain and simple to Graham, and Bettie could understand it. She would hate a fellow Private Eye to be so evil and abusing all the power they were given.

It was flat out wrong that Caleb Young and other senior cops hated gays and were going out of their way to punish them. This had to stop and now somehow Bettie and Graham had to prevent Caleb from ever doing this again.

Bettie kissed Graham on the head and loved the amazing smell of his manly aftershave that left a refreshing taste in her mouth.

But Bettie had only two ideas about how to

prove that Caleb was one of the attackers, and both ideas sounded as bad as the other. Her first idea was to simply find the other two attackers and get them to roll on Caleb.

Yet Bettie knew that that was going to be difficult, even if they did manage to find the other two attackers, getting them to roll on Caleb would be impossible.

Or Bettie's other idea was to attempt to force the other homophobic cops to see Caleb as a liability making them give up their support for him. Then Caleb would become very touchable and nowhere near as immortal as he believed he actually was.

"We need to stop him," Graham said, standing up and walking over to the whiteboards.

"What is The Cops and Justice bar?" Bettie asked.

Graham rolled his eyes. "It's the cop bar in Canterbury. All the senior officers go there and if you're racist, homophobic and islamophobic. Then you are really welcomed because you have *proper* cop attitudes,"

Bettie just wanted to make it better for Graham. She could see it clearly how much this was all paining him.

"And the worse thing Bet," Graham said, "is it's where all the power players go. If you want to go up the ranks quicker, then you need to have those attitudes and go to that bar,"

"Ever been?" Bettie asked.

Graham shot her a sideways glance.

"Sorry," Bettie said.

"How do we proof Caleb was an attacker?" Graham asked.

Bettie picked up her laptop from the coffee table and started to search nearby security cameras using Graham's login.

Then her screen went black and she was logged out of the network.

"Babe?" Bettie asked.

"What?"

Bettie showed him the screen.

"Is it possible Caleb disabled the remote log in on your police account?" Bettie asked.

Graham punched the air. "Bastard. The only place I could access the cameras now would be my desk. But I'm off duty so they would never allow me back into the building,"

Bettie laughed. She hadn't realised before now how pathetic Caleb actually was, was he really so scared of Graham and what he would fine that he would seriously block Graham from investigating?

"Our two homeless witnesses have been arrested. We cannot access cameras-" Graham said.

"Actually," Bettie said, "*you* cannot access cameras,"

Graham frowned a little. "How can you?"

Bettie looked back at her laptop and logged into the Dark Web.

"Well Private Eyes and ones that are licensed by

the British Private Eye Federation, don't play by cops rules, and there are strict laws on arresting us,"

Graham gasped. "Seriously?"

Bettie nodded. "Yep, after all the times corrupt and innocent cops arrested, harassed and falsely imprisoned Private Eyes. The Federation lobbied the government and they passed The Private Eye Act 2015,"

Bettie loved that little fact, but she had no doubt Caleb would try to arrest her. Yet that would be that mistake from what she remembered about the Federation, the President really loved her so Bettie hoped if she got arrested then the entire political force of the Federation would be thrown at the police.

"What you looking at?" Graham asked.

Bettie clicked onto the Canterbury High Street Cameras that various Dark Web hackers were streaming and Bettie started talking to a hacker about showing her footage from last night.

"Bet, what you looking at?"

Bettie smiled. "Babe I love you. You don't want to know,"

After promising to consider the name Theodore (a name Bettie hated), the hacker showed Bettie the camera footage from last night.

It showed actually what the homeless men said. Bettie could clearly see them walking back from a fast food restaurant and Sean and Harry were laughing and really enjoying their time together.

Bettie paused the footage. She wasn't sure if she was ready to see it.

Graham sat down next to her and Bettie played the footage.

Three men ran from the high street towards Harry and Sean. Bettie could see the knife and pipe. And another man.

The footage went black.

"What's happened?" Graham asked.

Bettie typed in that question to the hacker who said there was no more footage. The camera had stopped working at that moment.

Bettie turned on the voice function of the Dark Web chat.

"Can you print off the last five frames for me please? And try to recover the missing footage?" Bettie asked.

Graham laughed. "How can this hacker print stuff for you?"

Bettie laughed as she heard her printer working upstairs.

"Detective Adams behave," a very deep computerised voice said. "Of course Miss English, I like Sean. I'll have the results for free as soon as possible,"

Bettie logged out of the Dark Web, and kissed Graham on the cheek.

"You really are full of surprises," Graham said.

Someone pounded on the door.

"Bettie English! Open up! This is the police!"

Caleb shouted.

Bettie laughed. This was fucking typical.

Bettie gestured to Graham to stall him and Graham rushed off to the door.

Bettie jumped up and carried her laptop into her own massive kitchen and went over to the floor-to-ceiling silver fridge and opened it.

Thankfully she had put in a force bottom years ago in case this ever happened. So Bettie took out the draw full of biting cold vegetables, popped up on the bottom and placed her laptop safely inside.

Then she put everything back in and made sure it looked like nothing had ever been out of place.

Bettie rushed back to the front door.

Graham opened it.

Caleb was standing there smiling with three uniformed cops. Bettie instantly recognised two of them from earlier, the same male uniforms who had arrested the homeless men.

"Bettie English I am arresting you for criminal intent, trespassing and hiding evidence," Caleb Young said.

"Take me!" Graham shouted.

Bettie laughed. "Call the Federation Graham,"

"Piss off Detective Adams," Caleb said, "the only reason I've not arrested you is because there's more paperwork and press if I arrest a cop,"

Bettie really laughed at that. He really had no idea how much paperwork was involved in arresting a Private Eye on fake charges.

The two uniformed cops handcuffed Bettie and Bettie felt her twins kick inside her like this was going to be the start of some fun roller coaster.

And it was.

Bettie wasn't scared.

She knew this was the start of something fun.

She was going to bring Caleb Young's career crashing down.

CHAPTER 12
17th June 2022
Canterbury, England

Graham was utterly shocked at the political power of the Private Eye Federation. They were some of the most powerful people in politics in turned out and their influence was… almost dangerous.

As soon as Bettie had been arrested Graham had made two calls. The first to the Federation and he was still shocked that in less an hour the President David Osborne had driven down to Canterbury from London.

Then the second phone call was to an old friend, Maya Jean of NGD News but that had only ended in a voicemail by Graham. But hopefully she would pick up and camp out the police station for Bettie's release.

Graham was so impressed with David Osborne that he was now standing in a large metal interrogation room with a metal table, two chairs and two-way mirror.

The smell of burnt coffee, urine and even blood filled the interrogation room, and Graham knew exactly who was behind the mirror. He knew that Caleb and his girlfriend now Detective Serenity Simpson were looking at him.

And he wanted them to look.

Graham wanted them to look at him and his friends stop their corrupting influence.

David stood next to Graham, and considering all the Presidents and really posh, senior people he knew were all overweight, ugly and arrogant people. David was actually a breath of fresh air in his tight blue suit, very slim body and his grey hair was perfectly combed.

The interrogator room door opened and Bettie walked in wearing handcuffs, but just like normal she looked so beautiful, perfect and like she was in complete control.

Her entire face lit up when she saw David. She clearly hadn't been expecting the President to turn up for her.

From what Graham could understand there was a bit of history between the two. Bettie was one of the UK's best private eyes after all, and the President often called her to pick her brain on regulations and anything they wanted to lobby parliament for.

Two uniformed officers forced Bettie to sit at the table, and then Caleb and Serenity walked in. Caleb sat down directly opposite Bettie.

Graham hated both of them. He couldn't believe Serenity had jumped from a uniformed officer in March to now being a Detective so quickly. It was amazing how a little proper attitude can make you raise in the police.

Graham wanted to punch both of them.

David stepped forward.

"Is this your lawyer?" Caleb asked Bettie, like David was just another idiot who he could control.

David laughed in a very posh voice. "No oh dear child. I am Lord David Osborne, President of The British Private Eye Federation,"

Caleb smiled. "I did not know the Lords were interested in a group of amateur sleuths,"

Graham thought Bettie was about to slap Caleb. Hell! He wanted to!

David grinned. "Mr-"

"Detective Sergeant," Caleb said firmly.

"Mr Young," David said, "I will be clear. You and your Police Station are in violation of Sections 1 through 10 and Section 15 of the Private Eyes Act 2015. I fully suggest you release my member without charge or The Federation will have to enact Section 20 and 66,"

Graham had no clue what he was saying but he had actually heard rumours when it became public knowledge he was dating Bettie. Lots of senior police officers whispered to him not to annoy the Federation at risk of them releasing tons of evidence about police corruption going back decades.

Graham wondered if this was what they were talking about.

Serenity laughed. "So-called Lord Osborne. We are police officers and some made up fan club will not threaten the police,"

Graham really wondered why Bettie was smiling now.

David grinned and walked straight up to Caleb.

"You police officers are such dickheads," he said.

Caleb's face turned bright red. "Lord David Osborne, I am-"

The door exploded open.

"Stop!" an elderly man shouted.

Graham cocked his head as the elderly man pulled Caleb away from David.

Graham sort of recognised the elderly man who was extremely overweight and his jeans and shirt really didn't fit him.

"Sir," Caleb said.

"You are to release Miss English immediately!" the elderly man shouted.

Graham clicked his fingers. He recognised the elderly man as a sort of Second-In-Command of the Police station in all but name.

"But Sir, she is a criminal," Caleb said.

"Fucking hell, Young," the elderly man said. "She isn't a criminal and if you don't stop you'll be the criminal. Me and my friends will make sure of it!"

Caleb simply spat at Bettie's feet. "You're to go Miss English and the rest of you,"

Bettie smiled. "Actually,"

Graham went over to the elderly man and took the handcuff keys.

"I don't think I want to go until those two homeless men that you arrested are freed," Bettie said.

Caleb swore under his breath.

"Section 20 and 66," David said, looking at the Elderly man.

"Of course Miss English," he said. "We will release them straight away. Please wait downstairs and I will personally bring them to you,"

Graham kissed Bettie. "You okay?"

"Of course babe," Bettie said. "I knew you would come through for me and the Federation Protects,"

"The Federation protects," David said.

Now Graham wasn't sure if the Federation was a professional organisation or a cult.

"I presume," Bettie said, "you called Maya,"

Graham had no idea how she knew that, but he damn well loved her for it. It was great how they just knew what each other was thinking.

"Excellent," Bettie said, kissing him, "Then let's start up a media storm,"

Graham smiled.

This was going to be great fun.

And hopefully Caleb would start to make more mistakes.

Mistakes that would make his powerful friends

drop him.

CHAPTER 13
17th June 2022
Canterbury, England

Bettie hadn't had so much fun in ages.

But she never knew going in front of tens upon tens of cameras and telling the nation about how the police arrested a pregnant woman, broke the law and arrested two homeless men because they were gay felt so good.

It was so much fun.

Bettie laughed as she sat down on her sofa in her living room in front of the three massive whiteboards with Graham and David sitting down next to her.

Thankfully David had managed to clear his calendar for the day and now he (and the Federation's resources) were now at their disposal. And the wonderfully expensive wooden smell of David's and Graham's aftershave was amazing considering the urine smell of the jail cell she had been waiting in.

But on the way back from the police station,

Bettie had told Graham all about the information she had collected on Caleb from the other "criminals" inside.

It turned out that lots of gay, black and Muslim people had been getting arrested lately, but they were all of the same sort of profile. They were all young, men and either homeless or with few family members around.

It turned out that Graham had heard of this technique from the 90s and 60s. If the police wanted to target such groups then it was always better to target people who didn't have the family or resources to create a mess.

Bettie completely agreed. It was why she made sure the Federation got called and now NGD News was broadcasting the story every fifteen minutes, Bettie hoped that something would happen.

But the two uniformed cops were the key.

Since it turned out that all the people she had spoken to inside the jail cell weren't arrested by Caleb directly. It seemed to be that the two uniformed cops arrested them on the orders of Caleb.

Not only was that extremely illegal and outrageous, it was very unethical. But Bettie fully believed that Caleb believed himself to be so untouchable that he could and would get away with this sort of stuff.

"Who are the two uniformed officers?" Bettie asked.

All three of them heard the printer upstairs

working again and Bettie laughed. She gestured Graham to go upstairs and get it.

Bettie opened her laptop.

"I hope this helps," a man very deep computerised voice said.

Graham came back in and pins a group of photos to the whiteboards.

Bettie recognised five of the photos being the last five frames of footage she had seen earlier, but there were another twenty photos of the actual attack itself.

Thankfully hacker had been kind enough to cut out Sean and Harry so Bettie didn't have to see them injured or being whacked or stabbed.

"Here," Graham said, finishing putting up the photos on the board.

Bettie stood up and David joined them.

David pointed to a photo in the middle. "There. You can see two of their faces. It isn't perfect but I know the Federation got some new facial recognition tech,"

"How?" Bettie asked.

"Her Majesty's Government is very appreciative of our work," David said in a very posh voice.

"Can you try it?" Graham asked.

David nodded, took a photo and took a picture of it on his phone.

"My people should have it in an hour or two. The software's great but it will take time to clear up that image,"

"Thanks David," Bettie said.

She loved having the Federation involved, not only because it was a great organisation that always protected its members. But because David and everyone there was great fun to work with.

Bettie looked at the other photos. "I think this is the same two officers that arrested the homeless people earlier,"

Graham nodded. "Same. I know the officers and… they're normally good people,"

"Most cops are great," Bettie said, "but it's just the 1% we deal with that get cops a bad name,"

Graham smiled. "Thanks. The two officers are Eli Nelson and Toby Nelson. Not related by the way,"

"Do you think they'll turn on Caleb?" Bettie asked.

"I doubt it. Caleb is a DS. And remember the police is all about protecting and supporting each other. It's like every workplace, would you really turn on another Private Eye without solid proof?"

Bettie nodded. As much as she didn't like to hear it, she knew Graham was right.

"At least we can prove it was Nelson and Nelson that were the men in black," Bettie said.

"Shit!" Graham said.

"What?" Bettie and David asked.

Then Bettie realised. It was such a perfect crime. Caleb had completely used these two uniformed officers to carry out his dirty work, and they could only prove the officers committed a crime.

Caleb would simply argue that he had witnessed the crime and been too scared to tell them to stop.

Caleb wouldn't be punished here. It was Eli and Toby that committed the assault.

Bettie wasn't having that.

She had to find a way that proved Caleb was guilty.

She had to do it for all those gay, black and Muslim people in the jail cells.

And she had to get justice for Sean and Harry.

CHAPTER 14
17th June 2022
Canterbury, England

Graham couldn't believe how great it was to see Sean and Phryne again as him and Bettie sat on cold metal chairs next to Sean's metal hospital bed. And surprisingly enough the hospital room actually smelt rather great with hints of lime and mandarin filling the air.

But judging by Bettie's frowning face, she clearly didn't like it. Whether she didn't actually like it, not it was just her over sensitivity to smell because of the twins, that was another matter.

"Feeling better Sean?" Bettie asked, as Sean laid their topless in the bed with an IV drip still in his arm.

But at least the restraints had been removed.

"Yea and thanks for telling me about Harry. His parents spent an hour or two with me," Sean said.

Graham almost laughed at that. That could only go one of two ways, extremely well or badly.

"Did they say anything about Harry?" Graham asked.

"Na," Sean said, taking some deep breaths.

Graham really felt sorry for him. He had no idea how hard this must be for Sean.

"Bet," Phryne said, "you said you had suspects,"

Graham and Bettie just looked at each other.

"That's the problem," Bettie said. "We know who attacked you,"

"We just can't get to them," Graham said.

Sean frowned. "Who?"

Bettie rubbed his hand gently. "Two uniformed police officers called Eli and Toby Nelson. No relation,"

Graham went over to Sean's bed. "And DS Caleb Young,"

"That homophobic idiot!" Sean shouted.

Graham smiled and nodded. "In the police you get promoted in two ways. One because you actually deserve it. Two, you have proper cop attitudes and you cozy up to the senior officers,"

Sean shook his head. "How the hell are minority groups ever meant to trust the police when the police works like that?"

Graham padded his hand. Graham really had no idea what to tell him, because he was right, Sean wasn't the person in the wrong here. It was firmly the police.

"Why can't you touch him?" Phryne asked.

Bettie frowned. "He has far too many powerful

friends. If we go after him, he will be released without charge,"

"And I'll lose my job," Graham said.

Sean laughed. "I understand it. I really do. But this is about what's right, isn't it?"

Damn Graham hated it when Sean was right. Sure a part of Graham was far too focused on keeping his job, but he had to do the right thing and help all the people that people like Caleb targeted.

"What about the two uniformed officers?" Phryne asked.

Bettie stood up. "We can prove it. We could arrest them and Caleb would plead they acted against his orders and we only witnessed it,"

Sean shook his head. "Like hell. Caleb ordered those two to…"

Graham looked at Sean and smiled. Bettie clicked her fingers. Graham had no idea why.

"What?" Graham asked.

Bettie laughed. "Oh that's brilliant,"

"What!" Graham shouted.

Sean looked at Graham. "The attack. The knife and everything was aimed at Harry. They weren't trying to kill me. I only got stabbed because I tried to…"

Bettie kissed him on the head. "Exactly. I think we need to tell Caleb that Harry woke up and remembers something,"

"But why attack Harry?" Graham asked.

"Because of me," Rafael Rossi said as he walked

through the door.

Graham and Bettie bowed their heads slightly.

"Why you?" Graham asked.

"Because Graham I am not a normal businessman in Italian. I do work for the Carabinieri,"

"The military police?" Bettie asked.

Rafael nodded. "I'm not strictly here to see my son graduate and meet his boyfriend,"

"Neither one of us are," Bella said as she walked in.

Graham and Bettie smiled. "This isn't about sexuality, is it?"

Bella laughed. "Believe me Bettie. It is. Caleb Young refused to attack anyone else on the List, but he jumped at the opportunity to attack our gay son,"

Graham folded his arm. "What list?"

Rafael laughed. "This is why I was so rude earlier. It was partly because I was always scared of my son's sexuality making him a target. But I didn't want you English interfering with an op,"

Bettie wrapped her arms round Graham, and he instantly started to feel more confident.

"The Carabinieri has been tracking Italia weapon shipment for six months. They disappear like clockwork from different military homes on the mainland, the islands and throughout the world. Through my travels I managed to workout England was their destination,"

Graham and Bettie both clicked their fingers at the same time.

"Caleb Young used to work in Border Force until a year ago," Graham said. "Now he's basically like me. A Floater Officer or now DS,"

Rafael nodded. "Exactly, I am part of a Taskforce led by the Carabinieri and your weak Government has allowed us to conduct this op on your soil,"

"Why are you telling us this?" Bettie asked.

Bella hugged her husband. "Because it is wrong that your nephew was attacked because of our actions. And after other attackers on our taskforce members, we have no one left to turn to,"

Graham laughed. "You need us to help you stop Caleb. But how does he fit into all this?"

"Caleb still has friends in the Border Force I'm guessing," Bettie said. "I bet if we look into where he has been stationed and what department he's helped out at, we'll find it was always a department allowing him access to international shipments at the times of the thefts,"

"Exactly," Mr Rossi said.

"And that explains why Caleb has been trying to stop us investigating," Graham said.

Sean nodded. "He didn't want us to connect the attack to the smuggling ring. But what happened to the weapons after?"

Bella shrugged. "They are all questions the Carabinieri will ask after we arrest Mr young. But you are all right, Young is far too protected at the moment,"

Graham frowned. He hated that little fact.

"We cannot arrest him and extricate him back at Italia until you make him touchable," Bella said.

Rafael stepped forward. "So I know I am asking you a lot after everything, but can you please help me stop an arms smuggling ring? And help me get justice for my son and Sean?"

Graham and Bettie and Sean looked at each other.

They all smiled.

There was nothing else they would rather do.

"Shut the door," Graham said. "We have planning to do!"

CHAPTER 15
18th June 2022
Canterbury, England

Bettie hid behind the cold metal door in Harry's hospital room as she waited for that homophobic idiot Caleb Young to show up. Bettie hated him and she just wanted him to suffer!

The plan was apparently simple enough and Graham had anomalously leaked through police channels that Harry had woken up and wanted to make a full statement to the police this morning about what he had seen about the attack.

Bettie didn't know if it would work.

She didn't think it would, but they had no other choice.

All Graham, Phryne and Sean had said to her was to make sure Harry didn't get injured and they would handle the rest.

Bettie didn't know what that meant but considering she had to get dropped off home because the twins had drained the energy from her. Bettie didn't know what they had staged, planned or created last night after she was gone.

Bettie just hoped the plan would work.

The sound of a group of people stomping up the corridor echoed throughout the hospital room, and Bettie felt her stomach twist into a painful knot.

She looked over at Harry who the doctors had managed to wake up just enough so he could start breathing by himself.

Hopefully Caleb and everyone would just imagine Harry was sleeping and not still in a medically-induced coma.

Three men dressed in all black walked into the hospital room. Bettie instantly recognised two of the men as Eli and Toby Nelson.

Caleb wasn't here.

"How should we kill him?" Eli said quietly.

Toby went over to the door and shut it. He saw Bettie.

"Shit! We can't grab a pregnant woman!" he shouted.

The man Bettie didn't recognise smiled. "Don't worry so much Toby. This is just another dumb woman like they all are. There is no such thing as a clever woman, so no one will believe her,"

Bettie just wanted to punch him. She didn't have to hear this crap, but she didn't know how. Yet Bettie knew that Graham, Sean and the Rossi were watching her.

She had to stick to what little of the plan she knew.

But plans change.

Bettie had to change too!

"We can place the Nelsons at the scene of the attack," Bettie said, coldly.

It was great that David had contacted her late last night, explaining how the Federation's Software had worked perfectly.

"Miss English, I am Detective Inspector Riley Murphy. I have ten commendations for bravery and other rewards. I have saved children, women and criminals. No one would ever believe a woman like you,"

Bettie smiled. "People don't have to believe me. They can simply look at your record. Tell me several members of a Caberini Taskforce have been attacked, how did you do it?"

Riley smiled. "You women always think you know what's going on. You don't. There have been no attacks. There have been-"

Bettie waved him silent.

Riley laughed. "Nelsons wait outside. Stop anyone from coming in,"

Bettie wanted to stop them but she knew her family would come in the end. She just hoped they wouldn't be too late if anything bad happened.

The hospital room door shut tight.

Riley grabbed Bettie's wrist. "You women are stupid. You are just property but you modern woman never get that into your stupid thick heads,"

Bettie laughed at him. Hard.

"No wonder you and Caleb are such good friends,"

"Caleb will raise up through our ranks. He will be chief of Police one day, he will-"

Bettie just shook her head. It never failed to amaze her how stupid criminals were, they always believed they were righteous in their cause. But in reality they were always just sad little lonely men (and women) who tried to be tough.

Riley pushed Bettie away.

Whipping out a knife.

Bettie bumped into a wall.

Riley flew at Harry.

Bettie charged.

She didn't think.

She only acted.

She jumped on Riley.

He pushed her back.

He swung the knife.

It missed.

Riley grabbed Harry's throat.

The knife flew through the air.

Bettie lurched forward.

Grabbing the knife.

The knife sliced into her.

She couldn't let Harry die.

Riley turned to Bettie.

He started to force the knife downwards.

Bettie pushed against him.

She sunk to her knees.

The knife got closer.

And closer.

She felt the knife against her nose.

Bettie was losing strength.

The door exploded open.

Graham flew at Riley.

Smashing his fists into him.

Bettie grabbed the knife.

Throwing it away.

As Bettie raised her hands to slow the bleeding, she realised she actually wasn't as badly injured as she feared she was. And she stared at the knocked-out remains of Riley, she realised how lucky she had been.

Graham just hugged her. "No more field work for you,"

Bettie kissed him.

Doctor Lucas Bailey walked in with a smile. "My, my Miss English. We better get you checked out,"

As much as Bettie wanted to say no because they still had to find out how a Detective Inspector fitted into all this, Bettie nodded and begruntle went with the good Doctor.

But she had to find out about Caleb.

Something wasn't right.

And Bettie had to find out what was going on.

No matter the risk.

CHAPTER 16
18th June 2022
Canterbury, England

Graham was furious at the disgusting lengths this criminal gang was willing to go to protect themselves. Graham had to end them all.

Sitting on a cold metal chair in Sean's hospital room with Bettie and Sean and the two Rossi. Graham was still furious as he read the reports of the interrogations that so-called good police officers had conducted.

"Are we sure these police officers can be trusted?" Sean asked.

Graham just looked at the still topless young man who laid there on his hospital bed with two IV drips attached to him. Graham didn't even want to know why that was needed.

"Yes," Graham said. "I personally picked the officers to do the interrogations and they are far from corrupt,"

Sean nodded.

"If you allowed us to interview them we would know for sure," Bella Rossi said.

"No," Graham said, "these are English Detectives and criminals. They deserve to be interviewed on English soil by us, but I promise you I will make sure they are extradited to Italy if needed,"

Rafael frowned. "What do the reports say Miss English… I mean Bettie?"

"Nothing more than I expected. The Nelsons were simply following Caleb's orders on the night of the attack. They confessed to stabbing Sean and whacking Harry with the pipe,"

Sean's breathing started to turn rapid.

Graham and Bettie both held him.

"Deep breaths Sean. You're safe. You're loved. Nothing can happen to you," Bettie said.

"There is no danger," Graham said. "Harry is safe,"

After a few more deep breaths, Sean seemed to calm down but he still pulled up the thin hospital sheet around himself for some useless type of comfort.

"We have the confessions," Graham said, "but we don't have anything larger. How does a Detective Inspector fit into all of this?"

Bettie looked at Rafael. "You don't know who's in charge, do you?"

He shook his head.

"And Graham," Bettie said, "how old would you

say Caleb Young is?"

Graham shrugged. "I know his police file says he's 36,"

Graham smiled as he realised what Bettie was getting at. It made no sense why Caleb Young had still been a uniformed officer at the age of 36 then suddenly he was promoted to DS in the space of a few months. He had to do something before becoming a cop.

"You don't think he was always a cop," Graham said.

Bettie shook her head. "When I was with Riley. He mentioned that Caleb was like a god amongst men or basically. What if we're completely wrong about this case?"

"How Auntie?" Sean asked.

"What if Caleb isn't protected by all of these senior cops because he has the right attitudes?" Bettie asked.

Graham nodded. "It's definitely partly that. But you think Caleb build up a network around him because of his power in the arms smuggling ring?"

Bettie nodded.

"Oh," Rafael said. "Then that explains a lot. In Italia we knew someone called Chief Caleb and we always believed he was an international businessman who ran the entire operation. We thought Caleb knew who he was,"

"But Caleb is this Chief," Graham said.

Everyone nodded.

Graham was impressed with Caleb. He made perfect sense about how Caleb had managed to get such powerful friends because being a homophobe, racist and sexist bastard only got you so far in the police. Granted it could get you into a lot of places.

But after your "right" attitudes had gotten you as far as they could, Graham knew of only one other thing to get you power in the police. Money. And that was almost always from criminal activity and it explained how Caleb and Serenity had managed to be hired and brided by that psychopath a few months ago who kept Bettie trapped in her house for a little while.

"The question is," Graham said, "how do we stop Caleb?"

Bettie looked at Bella. "Tell me if the Carabinieri were to hypothetically leak the location of some weapons, how long would it take them to come to the UK?"

Graham loved that idea. They might be able to catch or at least track the stolen weapons back to Caleb.

Bella smiled. "Too long if they came from Italia. But I do have it on good authority that after your Brexiting your government would like to repair relationships between our nations. So your navy and ours are doing operations off the Kent coast,"

Graham laughed. "And I presume Italy would keep their weapons on a secured military base that someone with police and other more criminal connections would get access to?"

Bella looked at her husband who was silently laughing.

"Well my love," she said, "should we make a phone call to the Embassy? I think we have some leaking to do?"

Then Rafael simply looked at Sean. "I think we do my love. I don't want anyone's bambino getting hurt again,"

Graham looked at Bettie and she was beaming.

He was beaming too.

This was going to be great.

And finally they were going to catch Caleb.

Finally.

CHAPTER 17
18th June 2022
Dover, England

Bettie sat in the driver's seat of her little red car tucked behind some green bushes as she waited for her chance to grab Caleb and his stupid crew before they stole the weapons.

"Think he'll turn up?" Graham asked.

Bettie blew him a kiss as he sat next to her and held his laptop as they both watched the weapons that were carefully being loaded up into a large green military truck before they were moved.

"At least the Italians were willing for us to use their weapons," Bettie said, "but I wasn't surprised when our government said they weren't getting involved,"

Graham laughed. Bettie understood why, she couldn't understand why the UK government didn't want to help the Italians solve their case when that would surely repair any damage Brexit had done to their relationship.

"Are the others in place?" Bettie asked.

Graham nodded.

Bettie felt a tiny bit of pain pulse up her arm from her knife wounds and she realised how stupid that had been now. She was definitely going to be a lot more careful now.

The plan was simple enough. Bella and Rafael Rossi would disguise themselves and dress up as drivers who would drive the truck of weapons past Bettie and then somewhere along the route Caleb would probably attack them.

Bettie wasn't sure if the more secretive military base in Dover having only one access road was clever or silly. She felt as if she was about to find out.

"Bella says they're ready to move," Graham said.

Bettie nodded. Now she just had to be alert and both Bettie and Graham made sure their seatbelts were secured.

"So we have eyes on the truck?" Bettie asked.

Graham laughed. "You kidding me? Sean got so excited about the plan, he lent us all their drones and computer software that he had made for his Advanced Technological Engineer coursework,"

Bettie nodded. She damn well loved how excited Sean got about technology, it was probably why Sean and Harry made such a great couple.

"Yep drones online," Graham said.

Bettie looked at the laptop and smiled as she saw twenty little screens show up each showing the truck,

Bella and Rafael from different angles.

"They're moving," Graham said.

Bettie took a deep breath of the refreshingly cold piney air as she prepared herself.

It should take at least two minutes for the truck to drive past them.

Then all Bettie had to do was follow it from a safe distance.

"Shoot!" Graham said.

"What?"

"The drones. They're offline," Graham said.

"Computer glitch?" Bettie asked.

"You think Sean would create faulty drones,"

Bettie shook her head. Something was wrong.

The truck should have passed by now.

Gunshots went off.

Bettie and Graham froze. She didn't know what was going on. There was no sign of danger, the truck or anyone else.

But Bettie just felt something was wrong.

The ground started to rumble as something got closer, Bettie didn't know what to expect.

A large black SUV raced past.

Bettie recognised the driver.

It was Caleb.

"You aren't escaping," Bettie said.

She floored it.

Her car raced out.

Speeding along the straight country road.

The SUV sped up.

Bettie wasn't letting them get away.

Bettie floored it again.

Her engine roared.

It crackled.

It popped.

Bettie kept driving.

They were gaining.

The SUV got closer.

And closer.

Her car popping.

The car sounded awful.

Bettie smelt burning.

Graham hissed.

The car got hotter.

And hotter.

Bettie kept driving.

There was a motorway ahead.

The SUV would escape there.

Bettie couldn't let them escape.

Bettie couldn't let them reach the motorway.

Something banged.

Bettie's car slowed down.

Bettie kept driving.

The SUV drove quicker.

And quicker.

They were losing the SUV.

Smoke poured out of Bettie's hood.

Her car protested.

She could see the motorway.

They were going to lose the SUV.

Bettie stomped on the accelerator.

The car shot forward.

The SUV stopped.

Bettie kept driving.

Graham screamed.

The SUV sped off.

It was too late.

Bettie smashed into the back of the SUV.

Bettie flew forward.

The airbags activated.

The SUV flew forward.

Smashing into the metal railings.

It flipped.

As Bettie pushed the rest of the airbags away from her, she didn't even check if Graham was okay. She unclipped her seat belt and forced herself out of the car.

Bettie's legs ached and her two twins kicked in excitement as she staggered over the road towards the SUV.

When she saw Caleb pull himself out of the SUV and fall onto the road, Bettie frowned and she straightened her back.

All of this wasn't about being reckless and risking the lives of her two twins, this was all because she wanted to protect them.

Bettie never wanted her twins to grow up in a world where criminals infected the police and the very people who were meant to protect them attacked innocent people all because they were gay, foreign or whatever pointless excuse they offered up.

Bettie walked up to Caleb who was gasping and his arms and shoulders looked broken.

Bettie wrapped her hands round his throat and squeezed.

This excuse of a man had almost taken her nephew away from her.

This man had almost killed her family.

This man had almost arrested her and made her babies get born in prison.

Caleb Young deserved to die.

"Bettie!" Graham shouted.

Bettie looked at Graham who was getting out of her smashed up car and she noticed he was pointing to three green military trucks pulling up.

Heavily armed soldiers were getting out. Pointing their weapons at her.

Or in reality, they were pointing their weapons at Caleb and the three other men who were slowly starting to get out of the smashed SUV.

They were clearly British soldiers and two of them grabbed Bettie and pulled her away.

A moment later another black SUV pulled up with Italian plates and a very injured Bella got out (she had clearly been shot in the shoulder) along with five armed Italian soldiers.

"Gentleman," Bella said, "by the command of the President of Italy, you are ordered to hand over Caleb Young and his crew,"

The tallest soldier next to Bettie laughed. "We

ain't giving them to you love,"

Bella smiled. "You English had your chance to be part of this op. You rejected it. This is an Italian op and I fully suggest you hand over these criminals. Or I swear to God you will personally be responsible for a diplomatic incident,"

All the soldiers looked at the man who laughed and Bettie quickly realised he wasn't in charge, but now he had spoken he had become the de-facto leader.

"Handover them all. I doubt these foreigners could do better,"

Bettie walked away from him and went over to Caleb.

She smashed her fists into him.

"That's for my nephew,"

Caleb laughed.

Bettie simply walked away.

Caleb was caught.

His weapon smuggling ring was over.

It was all over.

CHAPTER 18
18th June 2022
Canterbury, England

Even now as Graham sat on a wonderfully warm metal chair in Sean's hospital room and him resting an arm on Sean's metal hospital bed surrounded by the amazing people he loved, Graham was still extremely impressed and rather shocked how successful the operation had gone.

Sure Graham wasn't a fan about Bettie smashing up her car, risking her safety and his too. But he loved the result and finally after so long and after so much grief, Caleb Young was finally behind bars and being tried in Italy for all of his crimes.

And thankfully The British and Italian Private Eye Federations had put enough pressure on their own governments to make a legally binding agreement that when Caleb Young gets out of Italian prison at age 70, he would be sent back to the UK and serve his prison sentence for masterminding the attack behind Sean and Harry.

It might not have been perfect but Graham was still pleased.

Graham was still extremely impressed that Bella and Rafael had leaked the information by broadcasting the weapon information on a "secure" police channel that they knew Caleb listened to.

It seemed so simple and like it was doomed to fail, but Graham realised that Caleb wasn't a normal police officer anymore.

It turned out he use to serve in the British Royal Navy travelling the world helping to keep the UK and its allies safe. So maybe once Caleb did know the difference between right and wrong.

That was a long time ago.

Throughout a bit more research it hadn't been hard for Graham and Bettie to find out Caleb had used his Navy connections to build up quite the network for smuggling and selling illegal weapons.

Of course officially the Italian government had seized all Caleb's assets because the UK government still didn't want to help out (Graham still didn't understand why). But somehow a few thousand pounds had slipped into Bettie's account, so Graham wasn't going to complain.

He saw it as compensation for Caleb's crimes.

And thankfully Serenity had been charged too by the UK police for corruption. Graham didn't know if she would get sent to prison, but at least she would never work as a cop again.

That really made Graham happy.

The hospital room no longer smelt horrible, disgusting or anything even remotely unpleasant. Instead to Graham's relief the room smelt of calming lime, oranges and even a few hints of lemon.

All around Graham Bettie, Sean and Phryne were laughing and smiling and enjoying themselves. And that was why this case had been so important.

This case was never about the senior police's attitudes towards sexuality, police corruption or anything like that. It was all about protecting the world, all the innocent people that Caleb persecuted because of some strange delusions, but most importantly this was about family.

The entire reason why Graham had fought so hard on this case was because he never wanted Sean and Harry to be scared and having to look over their shoulders constantly because some nutter might try and kill them.

And Graham really didn't want his children having to grow up in a world that hated different people.

Graham was never going to allow that to happen. He would always protect innocent people, no matter what they were, who they loved and what they looked like.

As Sean hugged Graham and thanked him for everything him and Bettie had done for him and Harry, Graham really felt some emotion move through him.

Not because it was great to be appreciated, but because now he felt without a shadow of a doubt that he was part of this family.

Before Graham had always been worried about being an outsider, a person who was alone and not accepted (or only tolerated) by Bettie's family.

But he was flat out wrong.

He had stupidly been thinking Bettie's family would have done the same as his family did to Bettie. But they were different amazing people, and Graham was always going to love, protect and be a part of the amazing English family.

And he really looked forward to expanding it.

Someone knocked on the door.

"Doctor," Bettie said with a massive smile.

Doctor Lucas Bailey walked into the room with a massive smile on his face. Graham couldn't tell if the doctor was happy about seeing all of them, or if he was just being his normal happy self.

"I'm sure Mr and Mrs Rossi," Lucas said, "will be here soon. I thought you would like to know the news about Harry as soon as possible,"

Everyone nodded. Sean crawled to the end of his hospital bed, clearly still in some pain.

Lucas shut the door.

Graham and Bettie looked at each other and held Sean's hands. Phryne gently rubbed Sean's back.

"Sean," Lucas said slowly. "Harry is awake and he has just returned from Neurology,"

Graham felt his stomach tighten.

"There's no easy way to tell you this. Harry did sustain some brain damage in the attack,"

Graham tightened his grip round Sean's hand.

"But there is some good news. Neurology says the brain damage is temporary. It will be gone with therapy in about a year or two," Lucas said.

Graham went to tighten his hand again but Sean shook them all free and he simply fell back onto his bed looking sad.

"Going back to Italy I take it," Sean said, depressed. "Never going to see him again. I've lost the love of my life,"

Bella and Rafael walked in the room arm in arm.

"Actually Sean," Bella said, "We aren't going to stop our secretive work with carabinieri and we need to keep Harry safe,"

Rafael nodded. "Exactly. My bambino will be safest here in the UK and with people who love him. If it's okay with you Phryne and Sean, can you please look after our son?"

Sean spun round to Phryne. Graham feared he might snap his neck.

"Before," Lucas said, "you make that decision. There is still brain damage that will require regular therapy in the hospital, because of three problems Harry has,"

Graham heard Sean gasp.

Bettie stood up. "What are they doctor?"

"I'm not a neurologist so I didn't know these were a thing. Harry's intellect is still outstanding, he knows and remembers most things,"

"But?" Sean asked.

"Harry has massive balance issues, he cannot speak all the words he used to but he knows them, and he cannot form certain types of memories,"

Sean nodded slowly. Graham just wished there was something he could do.

"He can get better with therapy though?" Sean asked.

Lucas nodded. "I'll wait outside if you have any other questions. I have explained everything to Mr and Mrs Rossi, but please come to the front desk later because we need to discharge Harry into someone's care so the neurology department knows who to contact about treatment,"

"Thank you Doctor," Graham said.

Everyone looked at Phryne. She looked panicked.

Bettie was biting her lip and Graham completely agreed with her. Phryne was only panicking because her useless husband John wasn't here with his son that almost died two days ago.

Graham knew he had to take charge.

He stood up. "Mr and Mrs Rossi, even if we need to wait a while until Phryne and John can discuss it all, we will take him,"

Bettie stood up. "We will. We can still look after Harry and I'm sure Sean will stay with us for a while and we have more than enough money to hire a carer if needed,"

"Harry is family," Graham said firmly.

Graham almost jumped when Sean grabbed him and Bettie pulled them in for a massive hug.

And it was right there and then that Graham knew he was always going to be a part of this family and he was always going to be loved, protected and cared for by each and every one of them.

And Graham was sure as hell going to do the same to them, and that all started by making sure Harry was looked after.

CHAPTER 19
18th June 2022
Canterbury, England

Bettie laid on her amazingly soft sofa in her office with her head resting on Graham's wonderful lap whilst her hands rested on her baby bump, and she was really pleased with how everything had turned out.

It seemed so strange that after the past two days she would actually want to lie here and Bettie was almost scared of hearing Sean shout out in agony again, but she knew that wasn't going to happen.

Because both her stunning Sean and Harry were safe and the bad guys had been arrested.

Bettie was still surprised at the scale of the weapon smuggling but it had made perfect sense, because Caleb was a horrible vile man who had used his attitudes and hate for others to manipulate those in power. And that was why homophobia, racism and all the other phobias were stupid.

All those people (like Detective Inspector Riley) might have felt strong, powerful and respected because of their commitment to preserving society's morals and all that utter BS, but Bettie knew the truth.

In reality all these men and women were just pathetic weak little people who were trying to be more powerful than they actually were.

It was just sad really.

With the brilliant cool summer breeze blowing through the window along with the most amazing hints of cakes, pastries and breads that would melt into Bettie's mouth in buttery deliciousness filled the office. Bettie couldn't imagine a better place to be in the entire world. Her family was safe, bad people were stopped and Bettie was with the amazing man she loved.

Thankfully useless John had finally decided to turn up, apparently his flights from LA kept getting delayed and whilst Bettie knew he was telling the truth, she still didn't care.

If John really cared that much about Sean then he would at least called, video chat or tried something to make sure his son was okay, and at the very least acknowledge Harry was part of the family.

But that was tomorrow's problem. Harry was alive and that was all that mattered.

Bettie stared into Graham's amazing dark eyes and she was definitely going to reward him for what he said. He had proved what doubts she had about him completely wrong.

After everything about his bitch of a mother who hated her more than life itself, Bettie was glad that Graham had proved he was a part of this family. Bettie might not have volunteered to take Harry in if it was just her, but she wasn't. Bettie was never alone now because she had her stunning sexy Graham who was always going to protect her.

Granted Bettie and Graham had both been shocked by Harry's inability to walk too far, his missing words and him forgetting how he got to places. She knew it would get better.

Because after decades of solving other people's crimes, mysteries and helping them, Bettie was more than willing to help Harry and Sean overcome their own problems, and Bettie knew that in a year or two Harry would be back to his normal self.

All because therapy worked.

Bettie wasn't hiding or trying to ignore the fact that the next two years would be hard, but Bettie wanted the two men to live in a way how Bettie wanted her own children to grow up.

She wanted her kids to grow up in a home they knew supported them, no matter what life threw at them.

And Bettie was prepared (or as prepared as she could get) for the challenges ahead.

"Harrison," Graham said.

Bettie gently pulled herself up and snuggled into Graham's strong sexy arms that she just wanted to hold her for the rest of time.

Or at least until Sean and Harry came back to the office after picking up a few things for their new room at Bettie's place.

"I want our son to be called Harrison," Graham said gently.

Bettie kissed his cheek.

"I want," Graham said, "our boy to remind us of this case. We'll still love him even if he gets called Harry, but I don't want us to forget what we almost lost, the pain and who we helped on this case,"

"There are other ways to remember," Bettie said.

Graham smiled. "Truth be told, I just like the name,"

Bettie laughed and playfully hit him. "Harrison English, or Harrison Adams. Both sound nice,"

Bettie and Graham just stared into each other's eyes as she smiled. She really did love him and there was no one else in the entire world she would rather have her kids with. Damn she was lucky to have him.

"Auntie!" Sean shouted.

Bettie and Graham got up and looked out onto the empty cobblestone high street of Canterbury with the sunset veiling the sky in bright orange.

When Bettie saw Sean with his beautiful blond and pink hair, she smiled. She really smiled as she watched Sean help Harry walk down the high street towards the car just like they should have two nights ago.

Bettie kept smiling because she really knew that everything was right with the world.

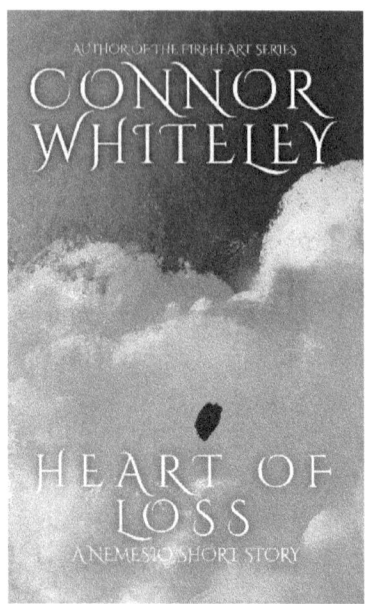

GET YOUR FREE AND EXCLUSIVE SHORT STORY NOW! LEARN ABOUT NEMESIO'S PAST!

https://www.subscribepage.com/fireheart

Keep up to date with exclusive deals on Connor Whiteley's Books, as well as the latest news about new releases and so much more!

Sign up for the Grab a Book and Chill Monthly newsletter, and you'll get one **FREE** ebook just for signing up: Agents of The Emperor Collection.

Sign Up Now!

https://dl.bookfunnel.com/f4p5xkprbk

About the author:

Connor Whiteley is the author of over 60 books in the sci-fi fantasy, nonfiction psychology and books for writer's genre and he is a Human Branding Speaker and Consultant.

He is a passionate warhammer 40,000 reader, psychology student and author.

Who narrates his own audiobooks and he hosts The Psychology World Podcast.

All whilst studying Psychology at the University of Kent, England.

Also, he was a former Explorer Scout where he gave a speech to the Maltese President in August 2018 and he attended Prince Charles' 70th Birthday Party at Buckingham Palace in May 2018.

Plus, he is a self-confessed coffee lover!

Other books by Connor Whiteley:
Bettie English Private Eye Series
A Very Private Woman
The Russian Case
A Very Urgent Matter
A Case Most Personal
Trains, Scots and Private Eyes
The Federation Protects

The Fireheart Fantasy Series
Heart of Fire
Heart of Lies
Heart of Prophecy
Heart of Bones
Heart of Fate

City of Assassins (Urban Fantasy)
City of Death
City of Marytrs
City of Pleasure
City of Power

Agents of The Emperor
Return of The Ancient Ones
Vigilance
Angels of Fire
Kingmaker

The Garro Series- Fantasy/Sci-fi
GARRO: GALAXY'S END
GARRO: RISE OF THE ORDER
GARRO: END TIMES
GARRO: SHORT STORIES
GARRO: COLLECTION
GARRO: HERESY
GARRO: FAITHLESS
GARRO: DESTROYER OF WORLDS
GARRO: COLLECTIONS BOOK 4-6
GARRO: MISTRESS OF BLOOD
GARRO: BEACON OF HOPE
GARRO: END OF DAYS

Winter Series- Fantasy Trilogy Books
WINTER'S COMING
WINTER'S HUNT
WINTER'S REVENGE
WINTER'S DISSENSION

Miscellaneous:
RETURN
FREEDOM
SALVATION
Reflection of Mount Flame
The Masked One
The Great Deer

OTHER SHORT STORIES BY CONNOR WHITELEY

Blade of The Emperor
Arbiter's Truth
The Bloodied Rose
Asmodia's Wrath
Heart of A Killer
Emissary of Blood
Computation of Battle
Old One's Wrath
Puppets and Masters
Ship of Plague
Interrogation
Edge of Failure
One Way Choice
Acceptable Losses
Balance of Power
Good Idea At The Time
Escape Plan
Escape In The Hesitation
Inspiration In Need
Singing Warriors
Dragon Coins
Dragon Tea
Dragon Rider
Knowledge is Power
Killer of Polluters

Climate of Death
Sacrifice of the Soul
Heart of The Flesheater
Heart of The Regent
Heart of The Standing
Feline of The Lost
Heart of The Story
The Family Mailing Affair
Defining Criminality
The Martian Affair
A Cheating Affair
The Little Café Affair
Mountain of Death
Prisoner's Fight
Claws of Death
Bitter Air
Honey Hunt
Blade On A Train
City of Fire
Awaiting Death
Poison In The Candy Cane
Christmas Innocence
You Better Watch Out
Christmas Theft
Trouble In Christmas
Smell of The Lake
Problem In A Car

Theft, Past and Team
Embezzler In The Room
A Strange Way To Go
A Horrible Way To Go
Ann Awful Way To Go
An Old Way To Go
A Fishy Way To Go
A Pointy Way To Go
A High Way To Go
A Fiery Way To Go
A Glassy Way To Go
A Chocolatey Way To Go
Kendra Detective Mystery Collection Volume 1
Kendra Detective Mystery Collection Volume 2
Stealing A Chance At Freedom
Glassblowing and Death
Theft of Independence
Cookie Thief
Marble Thief
Book Thief
Art Thief

All books in 'An Introductory Series':
BIOLOGICAL PSYCHOLOGY 3RD EDITION
COGNITIVE PSYCHOLOGY THIRD EDITION
SOCIAL PSYCHOLOGY- 3RD EDITION
ABNORMAL PSYCHOLOGY 3RD EDITION
PSYCHOLOGY OF RELATIONSHIPS- 3RD EDITION
DEVELOPMENTAL PSYCHOLOGY 3RD EDITION
HEALTH PSYCHOLOGY
RESEARCH IN PSYCHOLOGY
A GUIDE TO MENTAL HEALTH AND TREATMENT AROUND THE WORLD- A GLOBAL LOOK AT DEPRESSION
FORENSIC PSYCHOLOGY
THE FORENSIC PSYCHOLOGY OF THEFT, BURGLARY AND OTHER CRIMES AGAINST PROPERTY
CRIMINAL PROFILING: A FORENSIC PSYCHOLOGY GUIDE TO FBI PROFILING AND GEOGRAPHICAL AND STATISTICAL PROFILING.
CLINICAL PSYCHOLOGY
FORMULATION IN PSYCHOTHERAPY

A CASE MOST PERSONAL

PERSONALITY PSYCHOLOGY AND INDIVIDUAL DIFFERENCES
CLINICAL PSYCHOLOGY REFLECTIONS VOLUME 1
CLINICAL PSYCHOLOGY REFLECTIONS VOLUME 2
CULT PSYCHOLOGY
Police Psychology

Companion guides:
BIOLOGICAL PSYCHOLOGY 2ND EDITION WORKBOOK
COGNITIVE PSYCHOLOGY 2ND EDITION WORKBOOK
SOCIOCULTURAL PSYCHOLOGY 2ND EDITION WORKBOOK
ABNORMAL PSYCHOLOGY 2ND EDITION WORKBOOK
PSYCHOLOGY OF HUMAN RELATIONSHIPS 2ND EDITION WORKBOOK
HEALTH PSYCHOLOGY WORKBOOK
FORENSIC PSYCHOLOGY WORKBOOK

www.ingramcontent.com/pod-product-compliance
Lightning Source LLC
LaVergne TN
LVHW012112070526
838202LV00056B/5704